Home Field

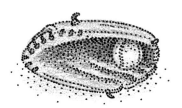

Home Field

DAVID SPOHN

Lothrop, Lee & Shepard Books

New York

To all the boys and girls of summer

First Edition   1   2   3   4   5   6   7   8   9   10

Library of Congress Cataloging in Publication
Spohn, David. Home field / by David Spohn.
p.   cm.   Summary: Matt and his father, just the two of them, play baseball early on
Saturday morning on their own home field. ISBN 0-688-11172-6. — ISBN 0-688-11173-4
(lib. bdg.)   [1. Fathers and sons — Fiction.   2. Baseball — Fiction.]   1. Title.   PZ7.S7635Ho
1993   [E] — dc20   92-5459   CIP   AC

The Saturday morning sun
shines into Matt's room.
There will be no late sleepers today.

Matt brings two gloves and a ball
into Mom and Dad's bedroom.
He climbs up on the bed
and gently peels open Dad's sleeping eye.
"Are you awake yet?" he asks.

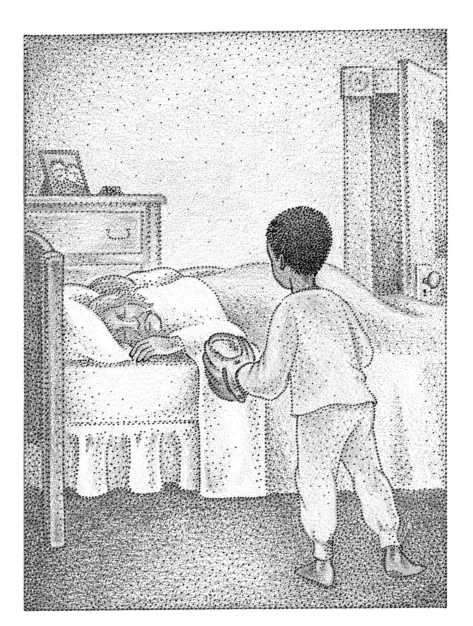

Dad's other eye opens slowly
and he crawls out of bed.
Today the morning chores
will have to wait.

Breakfast first—
two bowls of cereal
and orange juice for Matt.
Then he waits for Dad
to finish his coffee.
"Aren't you done yet?"
he keeps asking.

Outside, robins bounce
across the fresh green grass,
looking for *their* breakfast.
Matt and Dad cross the yard to the ball field.
By the time they get there,
their shoes are soaked with dew.

A game of catch
warms up their arms.
Then Matt picks up his bat
and digs in at home plate.
"Play ball!" he calls.

Dad goes to the pitcher's mound,
rubs up the ball,
looks over the field.
First and second bases
are bare spots worn in the grass.
Third is a maple tree—
there's shade for whoever
makes it that far.
Two more maple trees
behind home plate
keep foul balls from getting lost.

Deep in the outfield
the barn is the center field wall.
Its windows are gone now.
The broken glass on the barn floor
shows how much farther
Matt can hit the ball this summer.
Barn swallows nest in the eaves
like fans in the bleachers.

Dad looks in at the plate.
"Keep your eye on the ball and swing level,"
he reminds Matt.
"And try not to hit down the right field line.
Mom's everlastings are beginning to bloom."
Matt nods his head
and stares out at the mound,
waiting.

Dad's first pitch is high and wide,
his second low and inside.
His third is perfect. SMACK!
Matt sends Dad chasing high flies
and grounders to all fields.
A drive bounces into the chicken yard,
and the hens jump about like popcorn.
A long fly to right
sails over the flowers
and lands safely in the tomatoes.
Matt and Dad both sigh with relief.

Matt hits everything thrown at him
and waits for more.
A low line drive hits Dad on the shin,
then rolls to third base.
He hobbles after it and tumbles into the shade.
Matt rounds second and joins him,
sliding into third in the cool grass.
"Triple!" He laughs.

He can tell Dad is tired
and has almost had enough.
But Dad picks up the ball,
then pulls down his cap.
"One more hit," he says.

Matt digs in and levels his bat over the plate.
He lets one pitch go by, then another.
Dad peers in at Matt.
"All right," he says,
"let's see you hit this one!"
He goes into his triple
double windmill windup,
arms and legs waving in all directions.
Matt just watches and waits.

Then CRACK!
Matt's mighty swing sends a blast
to deep center field.
It hits the barn wall, high and loud.
Swallows explode from their home
in the bleachers,
swirling wildly above Matt's head.
Amid the cheers and commotion,
he circles the bases in triumph.

Laughing with joy, they gather up
the bat and ball and gloves.
Matt knows Dad has chores to do.
But he knows something else as well,
something *all* ballplayers know:
There's nothing better than a ball game
played on your own home field!